Fashion Fun

by Ann Marie Capalija
illustrated by Ken Edwards

HarperFestival®
A Division of HarperCollinsPublishers

Ponyville was buzzing with excitement. Sew-and-So was going to show everyone her latest designs!

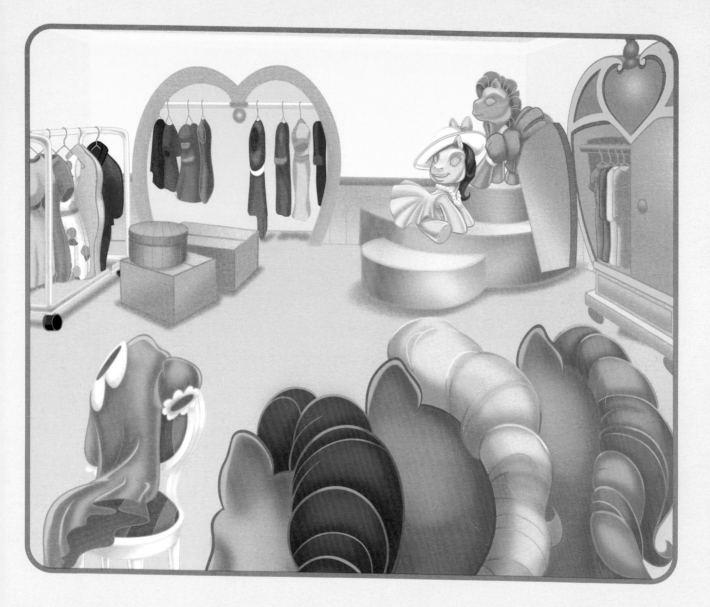

The ponies crowded into Sew-and-So's studio. New outfits and accessories were everywhere—in closets, on the backs of chairs, and even hanging from the ceiling!

"I really love this poodle dress," said Rainbow Dash.
"If I wore that I'd feel like the queen of any sock hop."

Daisy Jo admired a pretty sundress covered with colorful flowers. "These are just as pretty as the roses in my garden," she said.

"Your roses inspired me, Daisy Jo," said Sew-and-So. "And since we all know that April showers bring May flowers, let me show you my next creation." She reached into a big box. "I'm gaga over this yellow rain slicker."

"It's perfect for any pony who wants to stay dry in style," cried Minty.

"I just thought of a great idea," said Sew-and-So.
She buttoned the rain slicker on Minty. "We should put
together a fashion show."

"Fantastic!" said Fluttershy. "I'll take the pictures."

"And I'll create a special light show," said Sparkleworks.
Kimono and Wysteria offered to do the stage design.
Sweetberry and Cotton Candy would cater the event. *Yum!*

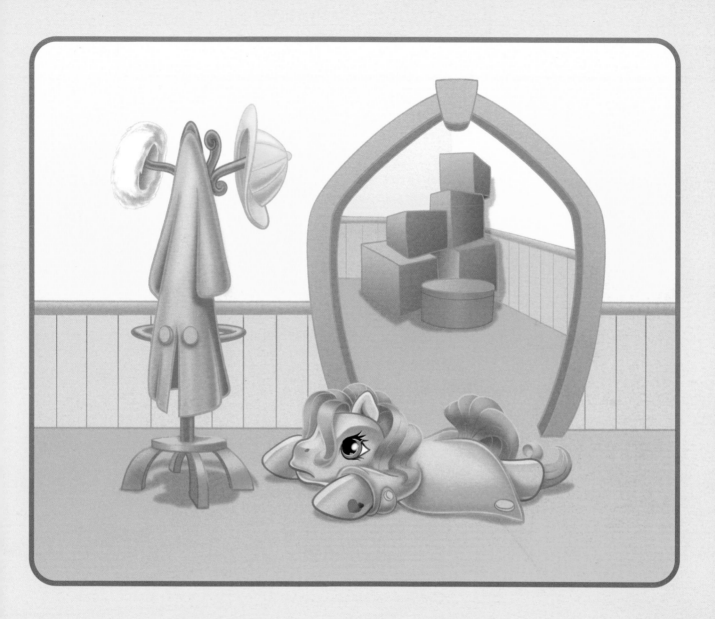

All the rest of the ponies would be models in the show. They began to try on all the different outfits. Minty was so excited she raced for a yellow rain hat and tripped. *Ker-plop!*

Oh, dear. Minty was just a little bit clumsy.
What would happen to her at a fashion show?

Sew-and-So saw that her friend was worried.
"You will be all right, Minty," Sew-and-So said. "We have
plenty of time to rehearse."

The ponies began preparing for the big show.
The stage crew made a long, gleaming runway.
Sparkleworks set up the spotlights.

Sweetberry and Cotton Candy whipped up some tasty treats for the audience. Rainbow Dash decorated the invitations.

Soon it was time for the dress rehearsal.
The models took their places backstage.
I'll go last, Minty thought to herself. *That way if I
make a mistake maybe no one will notice.*

"Positions, everyone," announced Sew-and-So.
The rehearsal began. Rainbow Dash danced around stage
with her skirt swishing from side to side.

Cotton Candy and Sweetberry glided onstage in frilly tutus.
Everything was going perfectly . . .

. . . until it was Minty's turn on the runway. She was more nervous than she'd ever been before. She wanted to be perfect like the other models, but halfway down the runway she slipped and fell. *Ker-plop!*

Minty got back up and kept on trying. But she kept on falling, too. The harder she tried, the harder she fell.

Minty's friends all encouraged her. "You can do it, Minty," said Sparkleworks. She knew Minty would be a great model if she could only be more confident.

On the day of the big fashion show, Sew-and-So gave Minty a surprise gift. "I designed a little something extra to go with your rainy-day look," she said, smiling. "These are special, rubber soled, no-slip, wet weather, gorgeous galoshes!"

"No-slip," said Minty. "I can't wait to try them." With her new rain boots—and a special friend like Sew-and-So— Minty knew that everything would be all right.

Finally, the time came for Minty's big moment.
She walked down the runway with confidence. Her friends
cheered her on and . . . Minty stole the show!